THE BLIZZARD OF 1896

THE BLIZZARD OF 1896

written and illustrated
by E.J. Bird

 Carolrhoda Books, Inc., Minneapolis

To all the good friends I met along the way who added a certain spice to an otherwise bland and lusterless workday world.

Library of Congress Cataloging-in-Publication Data

Bird, E.J.
    The blizzard of 1896 / written and illustrated by E.J. Bird.
      p.   cm.
    Summary: Uncle Tim tells in his own words amazing things
that happened to people and animals during the powerful
snowstorm in the West in 1896.
    ISBN 0-87614-651-5
    [1. Blizzards—Fiction. 2. West (U.S.)—Fiction.] I. Title.
PZ7.B51192Bl   1990
[Fic]—dc20   90-36831
                                                   CIP
                                                    AC

Manufactured in the United States of America

1 2 3 4 5 6 7 8 9 10 99 98 97 96 95 94 93 92 91 90

Table of Contents

The Blizzard

It all started with the wind that came sneaking across the mountains from the west and blew a few tumbleweeds into rows along the fences. Then came the clouds, black and rolling, filling the valley. And the storm grew with a great moaning, bringing with it the snow blowing hard and sharp across the land. The snow blew, sweeping everything—sagebrush, tree limbs, small rocks, pieces snatched from barns, everything not wired, lashed, or nailed down—before it. And it was deathly, deathly cold.

Starting on an afternoon in late October, much too early, even for a first snow, it lasted two nights and most of two days. When it passed and things were quiet again, the people looked out in wonder at the high white drifts and the dreadful damage done to the valley by the roaring winds.

The Blizzard

This was high country, mountains to the east and west and good ranches strung along the creek banks. These creeks fed a stream that wandered north through the cottonwoods, there to join a fair river. To the south we had the badlands, where our world dropped off into a hazy space of red rocks and twisted, broken canyons. We had a town—not much, but *our* town—and we had good people, and our valley prospered with hay fields and fat grazing cattle.

Now in a sheltered, close-knit place like this, you can see that everybody knew everybody else, and if something affected one, it affected all the others—like measles. If one person got the measles, everybody was bound to get 'em. If someone was caught up with a blizzard, why, everybody got his share, along with all the others. And we had our blizzard, and it became a ghostly milepost. When you talked of things or happenings, you thought in terms of either before or after the great storm.

So it was with my uncle Tim. This particular blizzard was the one big thing to happen in his life, and he could really go on about it. Grandpa said that Tim had been sent for a side of salt pork in the root cellar, where he was caught by the storm. He sat it out the full time, not even daring to poke his head out. Anyway, twenty years or so later, Old Tim was still ramblin' on about the big blow, and I, being nothing but small fry, hung on his every word.

After all these years I still remember his stories, and after the telling and retelling of them so many times, I'm sure he believed them all himself. So, here in his own words, are Uncle Tim's tales of the blizzard of eighteen and ninety-six.

The Echo

You wouldn't remember old Hank Ferbson, gone long before your time. He was a middlin' big feller, sort of stooped in the shoulders, lots of dark gray hair and a straggly beard. I remember him as bein' a dreamy cuss and messy around the bunk-house. The year of the big blizzard, that was back in ninety-six, he was with the F K Ranch as a hired hand. Come fall, after the main roundup, he was sent down in the red-rock canyons to flush out any strays missed in the big drive and bring them back to the winter range at the ranch. He took a pack horse and grub for two or three weeks.

Must have been four or five days after the storm when he come draggin' in with twenty or thirty head, mostly cows with spring calves. I was helpin' out at the ranch, and that night, after supper, some of the regular hands and I were talkin' with

old Hank about the can-
yon country. He was
an interestin' talker,
and I remember his
story about the echo. I'll
try givin' it to you just
like he told it:

I'd come upon this good
campsite and was feelin'
mighty pleased. Sittin' in
the shade of some old
cottonwoods was a pool of
water, a clear spring with
a trickle of a stream for
drinkin'. There was
plenty of firewood, and
a small arched cave,
set high enough in
the cliff in case it
rained, where I
could spread
my bedroll.

This place looked like it had been used a good many times over the years, as there were a couple of old fire holes and some pictures of wild sheep carved in the flat rocks by the old-time Indians. The canyons were hot, even in October—hotter'n a sun-blistered saddle—and I'd set there of an evening after supper, by the cool of the water, and play the old mouth organ.

This one night I'd just got set down when I heard music—mouth organ music! Lord Almighty, it was mine, played two nights

ago! It was bouncin' off the cliffs and sashayin' around the canyon walls—but comin' back loud and clear.

After fussin' round for two or three nights, I discovered the secret. I'd stand there and holler or play a little music, and it would take forty-eight hours for the echo to come bouncin' back—but only if I was standin' at the campsite. Anyplace else, nothin' happened. So I started prospectin' 'round and found a deep cave off in a side canyon.

The minute I stepped inside I knew I'd found the answer. That cave had been collectin' sound for years. It was hummin' and buzzin' with sound, but you couldn't make much sense to it 'cause it was all mixed up—like when a coyote jumps in a hen house. There was an openin', almost like a chimney, off the top of the cave, so I shinnied up and around the cliffs and found it was covered by a flat rock 'bout half the size of a saddle blanket. When I moved it, I could hear each sound by itself and separated from the racket in the cave.

So now, of an evenin', I would climb up and move the rock and set there listenin'. First I heard old-time Indians. I couldn't understand a word they said, but they chanted and beat their drums to some reed-type music. Then come the Spaniards and the early cowboys. One thing about a deal like that is that you didn't know who was talkin'. Oh, they'd mention names like Jack or Zeke or Bob or somebody, but you wouldn't know 'em anyway. One feller said that if you was to stand in a certain place and holler, it would take two days to hear the echo. Another thing, and this is real crazy, there was some old coot talkin', and you could tell he was old by his voice. He made a prediction. Said in October of ninety-six there would be one heck of a blizzard. I don't go much for predictions, do you?

After I told Hank's story, one of the hands, in the back by the stove, spoke up.

"The old feller was right, Hank. Too bad you warn't around. You just missed the meanest, rip-snortinest blizzard that ever tore through the valley."

The Cook

We was all at the store one night, settin'
'round, when somebody starts talkin' about
good cookin'. Nearly ever'body likes good
cookin', and nearly ever'body likes to talk
about it. Marty Brixer, who worked for the
B Bar C, started slappin' his knee and
chucklin' to himself, so we knew right off
we had us a story goin'. Says Marty:

Ever hear of a feller by the name of Rupin? Joe Rupin? Well now, he's the worst cook since the Ark. Mighty heavy hand with the salt, biscuits tougher'n a Mexican saddlehorn, and the stew he made—Lord, it was more like a poor grade coyote bait. Anyway, last October we hired him to cook for the fall roundup. You know, of course, that the B Bar C summers their stock high in the country 'round Three Peaks Basin.

We'd worked a couple of weeks snakin' cows out of the wild canyons at the top of the mountain, and started them down to the valley ranch. Left old Joe to clear up camp and bring along what was left of the grub and whatever else was layin' 'round. He had two horses—one to ride and one for packin'.

The second mornin' he started down the mountain and it began to snow. Soon there was a regular blizzard. This turned out to be our blizzard of eighteen and ninety-six. It was blowin' bad and driftin' all sideways, and every which-way he looked it was

white. When it got up to the horses' bellies
he knew he couldn't go much further, and
as luck would have it, he stumbled onto a
cave in the side of the canyon. After stakin'
out the horses where the trees grew along-
side the creek, he shucked off the gear and
piled brush and dry wood where he could
get at it and moved into the cave. Pretty
soon he had him a fire and a pot of coffee.
He was dry and snug. Figgered maybe he
could sit it out for a week or so.

First night he'd just got to sleep when he
was woke up real sharp by a great grizzly, a
she-bear standin' straddle of him and
drippin' snow and water. She sniffed him
over some and wandered to the back of the
cave, where she turned around a time or two
and lay down—watchin' him. First off, he
was scared. He wasn't about to make any
sudden moves. He built up the fire, and
the two of them lay there watchin' each
other the rest of the night.

Come mornin' he put the coffee pot on the

fire, sliced some bacon, and started fryin'.
When it was done to his likin', he throwed
some to the bear, wantin' to be friendly and
all, but she just sniffed at the burnt offerin'
and went back to her end of the cave—and
they set there watchin' each other. All that
day she looked mighty sour when he'd offer
her more of his home cookin'.

Next mornin' he started up the fire, and
the bear moved in and was lookin' over his
shoulder while he sliced and put the meat
in the pan. She watched it sizzle awhile,

then she shoved him out of the way and hunkered down by the fire pit. She kept watchin' and when things looked right to her, she snatched the pan off the coals and put it in front of old Joe. She cuffed him

one 'long side of the head, took two or three pieces for herself and ate it, makin' pleased little noises and lickin' her paws.

Next couple of days she watched him with her beady little eyes. Every time he was cookin' and about to burn somethin', or throw in too much salt, she cuffed him with a heavy paw, and he learned real fast. They got along fine till one day she slacked off and he fed her some burned biscuits. She was snortin' and howlin' mad. Throwin' him and all his gear out the front end of the cave, she sat there glarin' while he packed up and headed through the deep snow down the mountain.

After he got back to the ranch it took us three weeks of pryin' before he'd tell us what happened. Guess you know now about old Joe's cookin. Couldn't even please a hungry grizzly. We was all laughin' and thought maybe the B Bar C should have hired the bear.

The Avalanche

You should have known old Rene
Woodrupp. Now there was a character. Long
nose, wild hair and whiskers, and squinty
blue eyes. We'd see him only when he run
out of grub or when he got lonesome. He

was the sleepiest man I ever saw. Fall asleep even while eatin' his supper. Had him a shack, a donkey named Blinker, and an old mine up on Snake Creek. When he'd come to town, the high livin' would get the best of him and he'd wind up fast asleep. The fellers would strap him on his donkey and send him home. Sometimes we wouldn't see him for maybe a couple of months, but sooner or later he'd show up with his donkey for some town cookin'.

There was a long time, right after the big blizzard, when we missed him, but, sure enough, one day here he come—lookin' a might skinny and maybe a little hairier. Somebody brought him coffee, and we all set around and listened to his story.

Seems that when the blizzard hit, he was workin' deep in the mine. Had his rusty ore car full, and with old Blinker pullin', they headed for the openin'. Not knowin' that it was stormin' outside, he wasn't prepared for the big slide. Later he figgered that the

snow had built up high on the hill above
and had cut loose just as he reached it.
Anyway, the snow and the trees and the
rocks come crashin' down, coverin' everything, even killin' poor old Blinker.

Thinkin' it over, he decided things could
be worse. First off, he was alive, had tools
for diggin', plenty of water from some seeps
deeper in the shaft...and he could always
eat his donkey.

Well, he was a long time a-diggin'.
He was confused at first about the
time, 'cause in the mine he couldn't
tell night from day, but the donkey
meat was dwindlin' fast, so he
knew he was makin' some progress.
Finally he was down to one
leg bone, and he figgered he'd
have to hurry or he'd starve.
'Bout this time he discovered
the mine was full of bats, so
he started eatin' 'em. Ain't
much meat on a bat, but they

24

were plentiful. The next thing he discovered was that the longer he ate the bats, the more his eyesight improved. Stood to reason, he thought, bats see better at night, and so could he. Fact was, the mine was almost like it was daylight.

When he finally dug himself loose, it was a bright afternoon and he could hardly find the trail to his shack, but come night he could see well enough—so he headed for town.

He said after he got rested up some, he'd have to find him a new claim to work on and get back to prospectin' again, but he'd have to do all this at night 'cause his eyes now was only geared for the dark. He also asked around if anybody knew where he could find him a new donkey.

Next time we saw him was late the followin' spring. Said he'd found a great trace of gold in a basin, low on a cliff somewhere up in the Pipe Stone Mountains. He'd staked out a claim that night

and gone back to his shack.

"You won't believe it," he said, "but next mornin' I woke up and I could see in the daylight again. I could actually see! I was happier'n a coyote with a sack full of rabbits. Had me some coffee and headed back to the claim. Climbin' most all day, I was hard put findin' it. You know, things look a lot different in dark and daylight, and I'll be snookered if I could find her. Well now, I been lookin' ever since with no luck. Guess maybe I'll quit prospectin' for a while and go lookin' for bats!"

The Feast

Kent Stouter's Lazy S Ranch was on the far north end of the valley by the river. Here's where the storm was at its very worst as it came sweeping through the wild canyons directly from the Arctic wastes. Kent watched and waited while the gusting wind rocked the ranch house—and he could see pieces of his barn and outbuildings come tearing through the big trees out front and scatter over the garden. He worried mostly about the cattle, fat from the good mountain grass, and lately put to pasture.

"I'll go see if I can find the herd," he said when it was over. "Be gone most all day. Maybe look in on Old Shinbone's tribe across the river." And he took his best horse, the buckskin, and headed north, fighting the knee-deep snow and the new drifts piled high across the rolling land.

He found his cattle frozen stiff, some still

standing in the snow that swept across their backs. They had moved with their tails turned toward the bitter wind and had been stopped only by the deathly cutting chill and the deep bluffs at the river. A further search proved nothing was alive, and he crossed the big stream at the ford and saw the canyon where the Indians sometimes wintered. Here he found them huddled in their tepees, wrapped in their furs and blankets—and he searched and found the chief, Old Shinbone.

"Let's sit and smoke," he said. "I brought tobacco." And so they sat and smoked, the Indian and the rancher. They talked of many things, and how the storm had stopped the hunting. They talked about the sickness from the searing cold, and they talked about the hunger.

Stouter said to Shinbone, "Come with me and bring your people. Bring all your horses because I've got meat that will feed you." And they crossed the river at the ford and found the frozen cattle.

"Just leave one head, the one with the longest horns," he told the Indian. "I want to mark this place so we will all remember."

"You're a good man, Stouter, and our tribe will not forget you. Next year at this time, we will bring the meat, you bring your people, and we will have a feast together."

In the spring, with the blooming of the flowers, Stouter and his men were by the river. They found the head left there by Shinbone's Indians. It was, now, nothing but a boney skull. They mounted it on a

tall pole and set it so the sweeping horns and the vacant, staring eyes looked to the south across the valley.

October came and the day of the feast was set. You should a' been there! It was grand as any circus. There was wagons full of people, all dressed like it was Sunday. It was a great sight to see, women in long dresses, kids runnin' 'round like ants in a stepped on ant hill, and there were fires in deep pits. Oh, you should a' seen it. Old Shinbone had done it up proud. Had his men span the river with a bunch of poles and braces. They'd piled brush and dirt on top. We watched and waited by the skull till we saw 'em come.

It was almost like a parade. The chief was out in front in new buckskins and about five pounds of feathers, ridin' a high-steppin' white horse. Next came some braves in lots of paint. Then the women and kids come, ever'body on horseback, and the horses were of many colors, all gay

and gaudy. There were travois loaded with new-killed elk and deer—and a happier bunch you never did see, ever'one hollerin' and beatin' drums.

Anyway, here they come. Chief Shinbone made it across on his horse, but the men behind him come yellin' and stormin' on the dead run—rockin' the bridge—and then it happened. Ever'thing gave way.

Poles and dirt and horses and people and feathers and meat—ever'thing with a great crashin', boilin', screamin' thud went floatin' off down the river. Old Shinbone was sittin' there on his white horse with his mouth wide open.

Well, ever'body and ever'thing finally got untangled and on this side of the river. Only thing lost was a couple of horses and all the meat.

The chief, you could see, was mighty upset, but Stouter took it all in stride, just as if somethin' like this was an ever'day happenin'. He called some of his men to fetch three fat steers so we could get on with the feastin'.

One thing I saw, and I'll never forget, was Old Shinbone and Stouter settin' in the shade of a wagon, and I heard the old chief say, "Stouter, you're a good man."

Doin's at Grouse Creek

Sanya Swanner, now there was a gal. Big gray eyes, dark hair, pert nose, and on the shy side of five feet high. Any man who would come flat out and guess a woman's age is a fool, but I would say she was still in her prime. Somewhere along the line her husband was killed when he tangled with a hay derrick. He must have been a good provider, as he left her full owner of the Double S Ranch on Grouse Creek, where she raised fine horses and a few white-faced Hereford cattle.

Sanya drove a handsome dark green buggy with handsomer, high-steppin' matched bays out front, and she caused some flutter among the town gals with her fine clothes and how she wore 'em. Most of her land was in hay, and the young fellers would come flockin' at hay time. Some said she set a good table, but I'm sure there were other and better reasons. I had an eye on her myself once—before I was married. There was a son named James, maybe fourteen or fifteen at the time. She called him Jimmy.

People in the valley always think back to

that day in October of eighteen and ninety-six. The mornin' had started all mild and sunny, but the clouds were rollin' in when young Jimmy started home with the horses. He'd been sent to pick up ten brood mares at Christie's Crooked C Ranch, and he was drivin' them fast, with the old bell-mare out in front. This was a man's job, and he wondered if his mother would worry.

He was movin' right along, makin' good time, when the breeze picked up and the dark clouds moved in from the west. It grew colder, and a light snow started blowin' across the road. He could see the old mare shake her head and quicken the pace. Harder and harder the wind blew as it shifted more to the north—and he cinched his collar up tight at the neck as the sharp snow beat against his face.

His own horse, the black gelding, was movin' good, but the saddle felt stiff and cold, and it became harder to see as the wind grew. Now he could see nothing but the flyin' mane and the stiff ears of his own black horse as the whole world become a swirlin', blindin' white. And it was a much different world now, with nothin' firm and set, and a world with no directions. He felt, at times, that the bell-mare was movin' in a great, wanderin' circle. Follow the bell, follow the bell of the old white mare out front. He could hear it, now close, now far away, above the howlin' of the wind, and he hoped the ten mares between could hear it too.

Time, now, had no meanin'. Was it hours, or even days, since the big wind had brought the thick,

ever-blindin' snow? And he became aware
somehow of the dark hulk that loomed
above him. The bell had led him to a barn.
Whose barn? He didn't know or care, but
it was somethin' solid, somethin' he could
see and touch, and he felt the warmness of
it comin' to him.

Through the millin' mass of horses he
found the door and with frozen fingers
caught the latch and swung it open. Now
the bell-mare, the ten mares, he, and his
horse were all inside, and the door shut
tight against the wind. He found some old
saddle blankets draped there on a manger,
and with these around him he felt the
warmth seep in his body, and he burrowed
in the hay and went to sleep.

At Grouse Creek there was Sanya at the
window, watchin' the storm come sweepin'
up the valley, watchin' the tall trees bend to
the wind, and the limbs and the leaves and
the small things go flyin'. She watched the

driven snow that swirled like some wild thing that had fought the rope and broke the halter. She heard the limbs of the old sycamore tree beatin' against the siding of the house, and there was the sound, almost like wild wolves howlin', as the wind came down the chimney of the fireplace in the parlor.

Then the tree limb—big as a big man's leg above the knee—broke and caught the corner of the barn roof and tore it loose. And the rippin', tearin' sound of the barn itself as one whole side gave way and scattered in the barnyard. She didn't see the bull, the white-faced bull with curved brown horns, now free from the stall in the shattered barn, as it exploded through the front room with the crash of broken glass.

There it was now, crazy and runnin' wild, drippin' the wet from the storm and blood from a gash caused by the broken glass. Rippin' through the house, spreadin' great destruction. Broken chairs and lamps,

torn-up rugs, dishes scattered. All this Sanya could see and hear above the sound of the ragin' storm. And she could hear and see and smell the big bull as it ripped about the house. Now Sanya got the gun from the gun rack in the kitchen, and she waited for the time—that second where the wild bull faced her—and then she pulled the trigger. And he dropped. He dropped without another sound. Dropped to his knees and rolled over on the carpet in the middle of the parlor. And she sat there in the big chair, with the gun across her lap, and listened to the wind come through the broken window.

Doin's at the A-B Saloon

See that old feller—the one with the white hair and the cane, settin' there on the porch in the rocker. That's Old Bob—Old Bob Flowers. Use to be a gambler. Come here years ago, and was not overly friendly. No one ever saw him work, and people often wondered 'bout him. In his prime he was a handsome cuss. Thick black hair, parted strictly down the middle, steely gray eyes that never seemed to blink, always smilin'. It was the smile, I think, that threw folks off. There was never a spot on him, clean shaved, clean fingernails, the clothes, the shirts, the boots he wore—ever'thing was spotless.

And he was fussy. Wanted ever'thing to be in line, in rows, in perfect order. Like when he was playin' poker—those cards lined up straight as horses' teeth. Old Vilma, the gal that run the boardin' house where he was stayin', said when she fed him breakfast, even the eggs had to be in line, right down the center of the plate— and if there was bacon, there had to be two slices on either side to make things balance. "Symmetry," he'd say. "Let's keep things symmetrical."

On the night the big storm started, Old Bob was settin' in the A-B Saloon in his usual chair at the card table, with three other fellers from the town. They was havin' a friendly game when a stranger come through the door bangin' his hat against

his leg, beatin' off the water. He was a big man, blondish, with a four-day growth of whiskers and a black, wet coat.

"Ain't a fit night out," he said. "Name's Tucker. Mind if I horn in? I've got money." And he reached in his pocket and slapped a thick roll on the table.

"We don't mind," says Bob, smilin', and the big man pulled up a chair. It squeaked across the floor.

So they played. They played most all that night, while the wind blew and the storm whipped through the town. 'Long toward mornin' someone tried the door, and the storm came crashin' in and tore up things around the room—and the door was shut again. No sense in goin' home. And the cards kept slappin' on the table.

The stranger's roll was dwindlin', and he looked up at Old Bob with a sneer. "I think you're cheatin'."

Those were the last words he ever spoke. He slid his right hand down, flipped out a gun, and fired. Old Bob had seen it comin'. He twisted fast to the left. No one saw the quick hand to the belt, the quick draw, or the flash of the Derringer, almost hidden in his hand. What they did see, though, was the startled look, and the stranger slumpin' in the chair.

"I'm goin' for the sheriff," said the bartender, and he tried the door and faced the storm—and the wind turned him back into the room. They dragged the big man to the wall and set him in a chair.

"He bothers me," says Old Bob, and he

walked over to the stranger, set him straighter, fixed his mouth so he was smilin', saw that his sightless eyes were open, tipped the hat back to his likin', and stepped back, looked him over, took a cigar from his own breast pocket and placed it gently between the dead man's teeth.

"That' nice. Maybe you'll enjoy the game a little better now."

There they were all the time the storm was howlin', the players and the bartender, and the happy stranger with his still unlighted stogie in his ever-smilin'

45

face. And then the wind stopped and the sheriff come, and the judge come along too.

"How much did you win from Mr. Tucker?"

"One hundred forty-two dollars, your honor."

And Old Judge Kingston reared back and said, "We found out that this varmint callin' himself Tucker robbed a bank in Canyon City. While doin' so, he killed the teller. Also he stole the horse that he was ridin'. Since he drawed first, I s'pose it's a case of self-defense, so I find you not guilty. But...there's a law on the books, and it says that you can't carry a firearm in this town, and if you was to go so far as to fire one, I can hold you for disturbin' the peace, so I find you guilty on two counts. I fine you one hundred and seventeen dollars, plus twenty-five dollars for court costs, makin' a total of one hundred and forty-two dollars. Case dismissed."

Some time later Old Bob was heard to say, "I'm disgusted. Here I aimed for the third button down on his shirt. I was off a full two inches to the left. Maybe I feel sorry for poor Old Tucker, wanderin' through eternity with a hole in him that's so far off center. From now on he sure won't be symmetrical."

Goin' Out to Clean the Barn

Old Don Leeker and his good wife Helga had a fine ranch, high in the cottonwoods on Rainy Creek. Don was a middlin' tall man, a plodder, gettin' old, and not given much to hair. He had big, sad eyes always lookin' through the frames of store-bought glasses. Neatness, to him, was like religion. Ever'thing must surely be kept mended, painted, nailed down. Ever'thing must be kept in perfect order. Like Helga's garden— there shall be no weeds—and Old Don saw to it. All flowers grown shall be white, not yellow, red, or blue—but flat-out boney white. And things shall be in neat rows— and so they were. Old Don was like that even when he cut the winter's wood—had him a measured piece of lumber where he marked the limb before the sawin'. The house, the barn, the coops, and fences— ever'thing was painted white.

By October all the outside chores were done. The hay was up, the corn was in the crib, and Old Don was waitin' for the first deep frost so he could butcher two fat hogs and get those good hams curin' in the smokehouse.

One afternoon he says to Helga, "I'll still have time before it's dark to clean out the barn," and he put on his coat and started out the door.

"Guess I'll need my scarf and mittens 'cause she's blowin' up a storm," and he closed the door behind him and headed down the path with his back toward the wind. By then, the storm had brought the snow, and it was beatin' on his neck, so he hunkered down and scrunched his shoulders to cut the space below his hat. Then he saw the tree. The big, big cottonwood had snapped before the wind and was layin' split and broken on the path.

Long ago he'd built the shed, smokehouse, toolhouse, hen house, all in one,

with three doors all in line and painted white. And from the toolhouse part he got the saw, the long one with the jagged teeth. Plowin' through the storm he found the tree again, and he started workin'. He sawed and measured, sawed and stacked, and all the time the storm was buildin'. It was almost dark when he was finished, and he came to the shed to put the saw away.

The blindin' snow and the whiteness of ever'thing confused him. He found the door and threw it open, and the wind caught and slammed it, with a crash, against the siding of the shed. The squawk and shriek of chickens he could hear above

the howlin' storm, and the explodin' mass of feathers knocked him sprawlin' when they found the open door.

I've not been around much where there were chickens in a blizzard, but Old Don was, and he watched them scatter. He saw this one old biddie spring out and spread her wings, and the wind caught her, and without even flappin' a feather, she sailed clear over the barn. Two weeks later she was found three miles away under a sage-brush without a scratch—and she still had all her feathers.

Most people in the valley watched the storm safe inside their homes, lookin' out the windows at the brawlin' of the snow and cuttin' wind—but not Old Don. When the big clock in the kitchen said that it was mornin', he took his coat and overshoes, got his hat and scarf and mittens, said he'd best get out and clean the barn. And the snow and wild wind caught him, threw him hard against the garden fence. Like a

Sears and Roebuck windmill, broken loose from rusty bolts that held it, he made his way toward the safety of the big white-painted barn.

On his way he passed the pigpen and saw the snow had drifted, fillin' the fence part like a big white monster pie, and in the center the roof of the shelter was showin' like the plum to top it off. Don was proud of this little buildin'. He'd made it to house just three—the old brood sow and the two he raised for winter hams. Built like a big "A," on short posts with a planked floor spaced to let the wetness filter to the ground. 'Course it was painted white. Thing that worried Don now was that he couldn't see the pigs.

"Lord Almighty," he hollered. "They'll freeze. I'll have to get 'em to the barn!"

Did you ever try drivin' pigs? In a blizzard? He knew there must be a better way. So he somehow found the barn, went inside, got his team of horses harnessed, found the double-trees and the log-chain, and through the blindin' snow, with some hard drivin' and harder cussin', he found the pigpen. First off, he had to take off one side of the fence. This was easy with the team and chain. And with the chain again he made a hitch to the floor brace of the pig house, and the big team broke it loose and started for the barn.

All this sounds so easy—yet there was Old Don, with his frozen fingers, his glasses covered, his eyes waterin', battlin' the slashin' wind and snow. Ever'thing was white. There was no line between earth and sky. The trees, the buildin's—ever'thing was a swirlin', grindin' white. And he had the big team movin', he was sawin' at the reins, draggin' the pig house, with pigs a'squealin', headin' to the barn.

Thirty years ago he'd built it. He'd been there once or twice each day these many years. Painted it himself—so many times. And yet, somehow he missed it—missed it

in the blizzard—with a load of squealin' pigs. And the bank of snow gave way on the edge of Rainy Creek, and horses, and the buildin' full of pigs, and poor Old Don landed in a tangled mess in two feet of slushy snow and water. Even the horses screamed as they bounced and kicked toward the bottom, and the buildin' broke and the three pigs scattered.

He didn't dare tell Helga when he finally made it to the house. Didn't tell her how he'd unscrambled horses, harness, pigs, and log-chain up to his knees in icy water. Didn't tell her how the pigs had followed him like frozen kittens to the barn, or how he'd dried the horses with the hay, or about the horse blankets. What he did tell her was this: "Next year, sure as heck, I'm going to paint ever'thing—the barn, the coops, the sheds—ever'thing...red. Then maybe I can find 'em—even in a blizzard."

Miss Mary

Some towns are remembered for their wide streets, some towns for their fast horses, some even for their watermelons, but I hope that our town will always be remembered for Miss Mary. Miss Mary Lynn, she was quite a gal. Our town council had advertised for a school teacher, and here she come with her dark hair blowin' in the wind, and bright eyes lookin' straight at you—or right through you, dependin' whether you were fully grown or just small fry.

She took over the first day, settin' down the rules, and every kid in our one room schoolhouse knew exactly what to do and who was in charge. She did it in a nice way too. If some smart kid got out of line, it wasn't the usual rough-house thing with the big stick. It was more like, "Tim, go to the blackboard and write—fifty times—'I'm glad I am an American.'"

As time went on we got to really love her—maybe just because she was there. She taught us the three Rs, like all good teachers of her time, and she taught the little extra things like what's right and what's wrong, and how to be a good neighbor and a good citizen. It was a special privilege for the one who raised the flag each mornin' and took it down at night.

For thirty-five years she taught us— ever'one who was born or grew up in the valley—and she lived with us, as was the custom. Each family with growin' kids would board her for a month, each in its turn, providin' bed and meals and transportation to and from the school. In this way we got to know her, and she became like part of ever'body's family—of ever'body's family in the valley.

If there was one fault about Miss Mary, it was maybe she was just a little prissy. She was prissy in her dress, even for the days of long skirts that almost touched the ground.

No one—and I mean no one—ever caught a hint of a stocking above the high-topped shoes she wore. No one saw the lace on the multitude of petticoats, even when she climbed either in or out of a high-wheeled buggy. No one—ever—heard her say or do anything that wasn't strictly proper, and she would nail anyone to the wall with cold starin' eyes that wasn't proper in her presence.

Time come, as ever'one knew it would, that Mary had to quit her teachin'. "I think

it's time," she said, "that I must leave, and I'll be going home."

"This is your home," said the council. "This valley is your home. We can't lose you now, Mary, and we hope we've fixed it so you'll stay." And they took her to the new house—the one they'd built on Pigeon Creek.

Just over the bridge, and in the hollow by the creek, they'd built it. Old Lou Wilson had given and deeded to Miss Mary five acres of good bottom land. Ever'one in the valley had brought somethin'—lumber, bricks, nails, mortar, paint, shingles, door knobs—ever'thing to make a house, a barn, and some coops for chickens. They brought her a gentle, white mare and a new black buggy with red wheels. They fenced the whole five acres and leveled a place for a garden, and they filled the barn with hay, and the coops with chickens, and the house with furniture—each piece a gift from someone in the valley.

"I love it. Everything is grand," says

Mary. "Hope I live long enough to thank you—every one." And so she stayed and raised her garden. And the people watched over her, fillin' her barn with hay each year, and wood, all cut in lengths to fit her stove. Like Old Karsten Hansen said, lookin' in his pigpen, "Get fat, you porker. You belong to Miss Mary come fall."

"Only one thing I need," says Mary, "is a flagpole like the one we have at school. I do so miss the flag." And Old Lou Wilson made a quick trip up the river with his team and wagon, bringin' back a long, thin lodgepole pine, and set it standin' tall by the front porch of Mary's house. Now Miss Mary was truly happy, and she showed it with her friendship, visitin' the old and sick, takin' tomatoes from her garden to a neighbor, tendin' a child. All these were things that made her happy, and she was never happier than when she crossed the bridge at Pigeon Creek and could see her flag wavin' there, proudly, by her porch.

The blizzard came—the big one of ninety-six. Come tearin' through the valley. Two nights and two days it lasted, and nothin' moved 'cept things that were moved by the blowin' wind. And the snow drifted and covered ever'thing, and ever'thing was white and deathly, freezin' cold.

After it was over things came to life and moved again. Two old men on horses, each comin' from a different direction, met on the bridge at Pigeon Creek—and they looked at all the snow piled in the hollow.

"Good Lord, Karsten, you can't even see it," says Lou Wilson. "Can't even see the house!" And the house was really buried. The blowin' snow had filled the hollow, and now there was no hollow, for ever'thing was flat and white.

"There's the chimney," says Karsten, "and the top part of the flagpole. Hope she's all right."

"You go into town. Hurry!" says Lou. "Bring ever'one you can, with shovels. I'll

go get my team and scraper. We'll try to dig her out."

Within an hour they were diggin', founderin' in the snow, with white snow flyin'. Not much talkin', ever'body workin'.

"Look at that!" hollered someone. "She's alive!" And there, comin' up the flagpole, a little jerky maybe, like a flag they came— a pair of ladies red underdrawers with lace —wavin' proudly in the wind!

The Blizzard Party

I was very young at the time, but I'll always remember the blizzard party at Uncle Tim's ranch on Pleasant Creek. Our whole family was invited to come early and stay as long as it lasted. And there we were, sittin' and laughin' with Uncle Tim, Aunt Tiny, and all the cousins on the big front porch.

"I been doin' a lot of figgerin'" says Uncle Tim. "Been goin' over charts, readin' all the almanacs, and studyin' ever'thing I could get my hands on. Seems as though the weather comes and goes in cycles—so we're due, about day after tomorrow, in the afternoon—to have us a blizzard. That's just twenty years to the day after the big one of eighteen and ninety-six. This one ought to be a real honker 'cause she's been a-buildin' all this time.

"Now, you take the ninety-six blizzard.

Nobody in the valley was prepared, and she raised pure heck all around. This one won't catch me sleepin'. I been workin' harder'n a woodpecker caught in a bear trap, gettin' things in shape around here. Got ever'thing braced, lashed, bolted, and nailed down. Got the big limbs sawed off the cottonwoods. Got storm windows all around, and a new three-holer just outside the back door. Got wood cut to last three weeks stacked out back. Food—we got beef, pork, venison, killed two turkey gobblers and six chickens. Got a whole harvest of green stuff. Every day we're here will be like Thanksgiving, even if it's only the middle of October. This time, with all you folks around, I'm all set to enjoy it. I wanted to make a bang-up party out of this blizzard, so I invited you to come. We can set where it's warm and dry, with plenty of food. We can watch it through the big windows. This time I'm prepared. I'm really prepared."

Uncle Tim's ranch was a very special place. It was where he brought Aunt Tiny as a young bride. Brought her to the new log house. It sat on the north side of Pleasant Creek, in the shade of the big trees. First thing after gettin' settled, he'd built the big barn and the corrals and coops and pens. Then he spanned the creek with

a good bridge of stone and logs and finished the great white house on high ground to the south, where he could look across and see the barn and other buildings from the big ramblin' porch.

Next morning I followed Uncle Tim to the old log house. I liked being with him, and I think he liked me 'cause we laughed a lot and talk was easy between us. The old house was pretty much as he'd built it years ago. Just one room with a rough stone fireplace at the south end.

It was a very special place for my uncle, 'cause this was where he kept his books and papers and guns—things like that. There were snowshoes hanging on one wall. In

a gold frame he had mounted three medals from the Spanish American War. I think the thing I remember most about the place was the big bear hide on the floor—with its mean glossy eyes and snarly teeth. "That one there chased me all over the mountains 'fore I shot him. At one time it was a toss-up as to whose hide would be on whose floor."

The big day arrived, and we were all up early. We watched the sun as it cleared the mountains and scattered its light across the valley. It was a very pretty morning. "We'll wait and see," says Uncle Tim. Noon came with a few white, lacy clouds, and by three o'clock they had formed to blot out the sun. The wind stirred, and it grew black far out to the south and west, and the big thunderheads built up over the mountains. "I think she's comin'," says Uncle Tim.

It started with a few drops of rain that pecked at the dust in the front yard. And the sky split with lightning, and the trees tossed, and the rain beat hard upon the ground. More lightning and the crash of thunder, very close now, and the water ran from all the roofs in streams. And the creek, which minutes ago was clear and placid, was boiling and turning brown with mud from the hills. And the thunder rumbled in the mountains, and the big room would light up from the lightning like flashes from the brightest sun.

"It's a cloudburst!" cried Uncle Tim. And the creek was spilling over its grassy banks. Great rocks, tree limbs, and muck from the mountains were thrashing in the creek bed, and a huge cottonwood tree crashed and was carried to the bridge, where it caught and formed a churning pool that soon built into a muddy lake. And the water rose until it reached the log house and the coops and pigpens. And the bridge gave way, and everything went spinning down toward the valley—rocks and trees and logs from the old log house. And you could see the pigs

swimming, and there it went—the mean
eyes flashing, big teeth snarling, the bear-
skin rug.

"All I can say is that's the darnedest
blizzard I ever saw," says Uncle Tim.